TIGER IN TROUBLE

To Mum and Dad, who raised four little adventurers

ORION CHILDREN'S BOOKS

First published in Great Britain in 2022 by Hodder & Stoughton

1 3 5 7 9 10 8 6 4 2

Text copyright © Jess Butterworth, 2022
Illustrations copyright © Kirsti Beautyman, 2022

The moral rights of the author and illustrator have been asserted.

A CIP catalogue record for this book
is available from the British Library.

ISBN 978 1 510 10798 4

Printed and bound in Great Britain by
Clays Ltd, Elcograf, S.p.A.

The paper and board used in this book
are made from wood from responsible sources.

Orion Children's Books
An imprint of
Hachette Children's Group
Part of Hodder & Stoughton Limited
Carmelite House
50 Victoria Embankment
London EC4Y 0DZ

An Hachette UK Company
www.hachette.co.uk

www.hachettechildrens.co.uk

THE ADVENTURE CLUB

TIGER IN TROUBLE

JESS BUTTERWORTH

Orion

MEET THE
ADVENTURE CLUB

Tilly (That's me!) I love animals, adventures and exploring. I'm a member of the Adventure Club and I also started an Afterschool Adventure Club at home!

Anita is also a member of the Adventure Club. She loves planning and organising activities to look after the environment and care for endangered animals.

Leo is the third member of the Adventure Club. He doesn't like creepy crawlies or the dark but has bucketsful of courage.

Charlotte is my best friend and a member of the Afterschool Adventure Club. She loves dogs and adopted a giant puppy called Jupiter!

Julia is the leader of the Adventure Club, a medic, and an expedition leader. She's passionate about teaching young people about endangered animals.

Steve is the Adventure Club vet and an expedition leader. He never goes anywhere without his vet kit bag in case there's an emergency!

Rhyah and Adi are members of the tiger team in India!

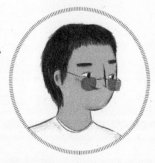

Hello! My name is Tilly and this is my adventure notebook! I'm part of an **AMAZING** group called the Adventure Club — we get to go all around the world and help animals. A few months ago, we went to Nepal and rescued red pandas. They were sooo cute!

There's just one problem. The next Adventure Club trip isn't for months! It feels like a lifetime away! What am I going to do this summer?

School, Thursday, 11am

It's the last day of school and everyone is moaning to Ms Perry about having to do homework over summer. Ms Perry wants us to choose our own project — we can create, build or make something. I'm secretly excited about it. For my project I'm going to create an adventure notebook — right here! I **LOVE** writing in my notebook anyway ... even if I don't know exactly what I'm going to be writing about this summer yet.

Earlier, I told Ms Perry about my adventure notebook plans. I bounced up and down on my toes and said, 'I hope I get to go on adventures that are very bold and daring and involve **LOTS** of animals!'

Ms Perry raised her pen to her lips, thinking. 'I thought the next Adventure Club trip wasn't until the beginning of next spring.'

'I can't wait that long!' I replied. 'I'm going to go in search of the **BEST** adventures now.'

'I hope your adventures aren't *too* risky, Tilly,' said Ms Perry.

'We'll see,' I replied and did a little twirl on the spot.

I used to think that adventures would never happen to someone like me. But then out of **NOWHERE** the Adventure Club changed my **ENTIRE** life!

Things about me:
- My favourite animals are red pandas, tigers, bees and butterflies.
- I have a pet cat called Marigold.
- Last term I won a place in the Adventure Club.
- That's how I got to travel to Nepal, with the other adventurers Leo and Anita, to help

protect endangered red pandas. It was **THE BEST WEEK EVER!**

- When I got back home I started an Afterschool Adventure Club. We planted a bee and butterfly garden and made a living willow-house HQ on the school field!

Some of my most recent adventures include:
- Watching a bee crawl around on the exact flowers that I planted myself. (I had to be **REALLY** restrained and not get too close.)
- Pruning the willow-house (which means cutting its branches so that it can grow properly). I had to be **EXTRA** careful with the razor-sharp hand shears.
- Walking my best friend Charlotte's dog, Jupiter. This doesn't sound very exciting but Jupiter is **HUGE** and it took a lot of strength to keep

him from running off when he saw another dog.
(He **LOVES** other dogs.)

Willow-house HQ, after school
When I first started going to this school last year I
didn't know anyone, but now I have lots of friends,
mainly because of the Afterschool Adventure Club.
We've had seven meetings and our willow-house HQ has
already grown into a dome shape and now has bright
green leaves which block the heat but still let in lots
of light.

Today was the last meeting before the holidays. It
was warm and sunny and we were all sitting in the
willow-house. I had my notebook open just in case
I needed to make any notes. The air smelled of
freshly cut grass.

There were six of us at the meeting: me,
Charlotte, Amira, Mo, Oliver and George.

Charlotte sighed loudly.

'I wish we could keep the Afterschool
Adventure Club going over the holidays,' she said
as she leant on her hand.

'Me too,' I said.

'I thought I'd be excited about the holidays,' said Oliver. 'But I don't want to leave the Afterschool Adventure Club HQ.'

'I'm going to miss watching the butterflies SO much,' I added.

'Maybe we can sneak in and still use the willow-house,' suggested Charlotte.

'I already asked Ms Perry and she said that we definitely weren't allowed to do that,' I said and laid back with my head resting against the grass. I looked up through the holes in the roof of the willow-house. 'She said we had to be patient.'

Being patient is one of the hardest things **EVER**. Sometimes, I can't even sit still to wait for the end-of-class bell to ring.

Other times I find it challenging to be patient:

- Waiting for the bus when it's raining.

- Waiting for dinner when I'm hungry.
- Waiting for my birthday when it's the week before.

Ms Perry popped her head in the entrance. 'It's almost time to go home,' she said.

'But we don't want to!' said Charlotte.

'We could camp out here?' asked Amira, hopefully.

'Maybe next term,' said Ms Perry. She had her 'don't get your hopes up' expression.

'But who's going to look after the bee and flower garden while we're gone?' asked George.

'The caretaker and gardener are under strict instructions and they know exactly what to do,' Ms Perry said. She looked at her watch. 'Five more minutes and then your parents will be here.' Her head disappeared.

'Do you think they know to record the butterflies that they see?' asked Charlotte.

'I hadn't thought of that!' I replied, sitting up. We'd been recording and drawing the types of butterflies that visit the garden and we were all hoping to have a special one visit from the treetops. The purple emperor butterfly!

'Let's leave them a note! It can be our last Afterschool Adventure Club mission!' I said.

'Yes!' said everyone together.

I scribbled a note in my adventure notebook, tore it out, and pinned it underneath the bee hotel, where it wouldn't get wet. It said:

This garden belongs to the Afterschool Adventure Club. Please record on paper if you see this butterfly — they are very rare!

Then I hugged Charlotte tightly. I couldn't wait to see her when she got back from her camping holiday.

Home, just before bed

As soon as I got home this afternoon, I checked the post. I'm waiting for a very **IMPORTANT** letter. But there was only:

- A boring-looking letter for Dad
- A takeaway menu
- Some supermarket vouchers
- And **NOTHING** for me.

I was getting worried.

See, for my birthday this year, I adopted a tiger. (That doesn't mean that I get to keep a tiger like a pet by the way, but I do get to help protect one in the wild!)

My birthday present included this letter from the tiger I adopted:

Dear Tilly,

My name is Tara and I live in a national park in south-west India.

Some things about me:

I'm five months old and I live with my mother.

I'm one of the last Bengal tigers. There are fewer than 3,000 left of us in the wild.

When I'm an adult you'll be able to hear my roar from two miles away.

I live for around eight to ten years.

I could grow to be up to nine feet long, including my tail.

I have a unique set of stripes. Tigers all have different stripes – no tiger is the same. Our stripes aren't just on my fur but on our skin too!

I have soft toe pads that help me hunt silently.

I can run up to forty miles an hour.

I'm a good swimmer and I love water.

Marigold my cat hates water. I had to give her a sponge bath once after she stepped in a cow pat. She was **NOT** happy.

When Marigold was a kitten she looked like this...

Tara my adopted tiger cub looks like this ...

They are both equally cuuuute.

But Tara the tiger cub will grow up to be wild and fierce whereas Marigold is cuddly (sometimes) and a bit of a scaredy-cat.

Every two weeks since my birthday the tiger reserve has sent me an update in the post about how Tara the tiger cub is doing and how many sightings of her there have been. They include recent photographs of her too.

But now a whole month has passed and nothing has arrived. No updates and no pictures – nothing.

'Maybe they're really busy,' said Mum.

'Or maybe the letter got delayed,' said Dad.

'Maybe,' I replied. But I couldn't shake the feeling that something wasn't right. And I was determined to find out what.

So today I wrote them a letter. Dad said that he'd post it via airmail so that it would arrive quickly. It said:

Dear People Who Look After the Tigers,

I know you are probably very busy protecting animals and saving tigers but I'm extremely worried about my adopted tiger cub Tara as I haven't heard anything for a while. Please let me know if she's OK.

Thank you in advance,
Tilly

I'm feeling **MUCH** happier now. I'm **SURE** I'll have an update on Tara the tiger cub soon.

Home, two weeks later
It's been two weeks since I sent my letter. It's been **SO HARD** waiting, but today I finally got a reply!

I knew the letter was from India straight away. It had a stamp with peacocks and Hindi writing on it.

I ripped open the envelope. I read it very quickly.

Dear Tilly,

Thank you for your concern about Tara. We haven't spotted her or her mother in a while but we will let you know as soon as we find them. In the meantime, here are some pictures of other animals from the reserve.

From,

Rhyah and Adi, The Tiger Team at the Big Tiger Reserve

They had included pictures of some other animals, including a lovely picture of a bird with a long tail.

But it didn't stop me worrying about Tara the tiger.

'What do they mean, as soon as they find them? Does that mean that the tigers have gone missing?' I asked Mum. This was **NOT** the news I'd been hoping for.

I imagined poor Tara the tiger cub, lost and scared.

'Oh, sweetheart, we don't know for sure that they've gone missing,' said Mum. 'The area that they live in is probably very large. Maybe they went to a new place?'

I nodded slowly.

Sometimes Marigold disappears for several hours at a time. I plopped down on to the sofa and thought **VERY** hard. Mum offered me some blueberries.

'Brain food!' I said. 'Thank you!' I tossed a berry

into my mouth, chewed slowly and kept thinking. Actually, I realised I hadn't seen Marigold for a while this morning. I stood up and tiptoed into my bedroom to check if she was asleep on my bed (it was her favourite place) but she wasn't there. It was time for some investigating. Maybe Marigold could give me some clues as to where cats disappear to.

The First Adventure

> **Objective:** To become an animal detective and find Marigold the cat.
>
> **Obstacles:** I have **NO** idea where she might be.

I put on my sunglasses and my wide-rimmed sun hat and began a thorough search.

First, I checked the pile of folded clean clothes next to the washing machine.

She wasn't there.

Next, the sunny top step of the staircase.

Not there.

Then Mum and Dad's bed.

But she was nowhere to be seen! I leant out of the window to see if I could spot Marigold. I scanned the garden for flashes of ginger fur.

Aha! I spotted her!

Marigold was patrolling the perimeter, prowling through the long grass by the fence (keeping an eye on the neighbour's dog).

I dashed downstairs and quietly sneaked outside, keeping a safe distance so that she didn't see me.

Marigold stopped and sharpened her claws for a while on a tree trunk, before leaping into next door's garden to drink the water out of the bird bath. (Their dog was **NOT** happy about this.)

After a staring competition with the dog, she decided to jump back into our garden, where she found a strip of sunlight on the grass to lie on her back and sunbathe. She stayed there for **AGES!**

I made a note of everything that Marigold did. After my investigation, Dad helped me find the Big Tiger Reserve's email address. (Dad said an email would arrive quicker than a letter.) I wrote all my discoveries in an email. It said:

×

Dear Rhyah and Adi,
When I can't find my cat, it's because she's gone off to drink water, sharpen her claws, make friends with the neighbouring dog or

find a new place to sunbathe. Maybe Tara and her mother are off doing one of these things too? Perhaps you could check.

From,

Tilly

Mum said they were probably doing everything they could already but I sent my email anyway. I'm so far away from Tara the tiger cub it was the only thing I could think to do!

The kitchen, the next day

I'm sitting slouched over at the kitchen table. I've just received an email from the tiger reserve and it is **NOT** good news. Mum gave me a slice of banana bread and a hug but I still feel sad. I hardly even feel like writing. I need to think of a plan. **QUICKLY!**

The email said:

Hi Tilly,

Thank you for your suggestions. I wish I could write with better news, but we still haven't found Tara the tiger cub or her mother.

The monsoon is late this year and they might have gone off in search of water, just like you suggested. We're hoping she hasn't left the protected tiger reserve as there are busy roads and villages around us. We'll let you know as soon as we have more news.

From,

Rhyah and Adi

My desk, an hour later

I sniffed and wiped my nose as I stared at a photo of Tara the tiger cub pinned to the board above my desk. My heart ached at the thought of something terrible happening to her. Busy roads? Villages? What if there were poachers in the villages? (Poachers are people who try and steal protected animals for pets or kill them for their skins or bones or teeth. I knew ALL about poachers because I rescued a red panda from one of their traps when I was in Nepal.)

Mum walked in from hanging out the washing.

'What are monsoons?' I asked her.

'It's a season where it rains a lot,' she replied.

'Oh no!' I said. 'How do I make it rain for Tara and her mum? They need water.'

'I don't think you can, sweetheart,' replied Mum.

'Mum!' I said. 'This is **TERRIBLE!** What if they

don't find water? What will they drink? How will they survive?'

'There must be water for them somewhere,' said Mum. 'I'm sure they'll find it.'

'But what if Tara and her mum get chased by poachers and get separated and then Tara the tiger cub is all alone?' I asked. I imagined Tara trying to look after herself and felt my throat go all tight.

'I thought they lived in a tiger reserve?' said Mum, reading the email over my shoulder.

'They do, but if they have to go searching for water they'll face **DANGER!** Look, it says so right here.' I pointed at the line about busy roads and villages.

'Hang on,' said Mum, reading over my shoulder and frowning. 'You might be slightly jumping to conclusions.'

'I'm most definitely **NOT** jumping to anything,'

I replied. 'Look, I'm staying completely still.' I froze like a statue.

Mum smiled. 'I mean your imagination might be making it worse than it is.'

I frowned. 'Now you're the one jumping to conclusions,' I said.

Mum laughed. 'Come here,' she said and gave me a hug.

'I just wish there was something I could do to help,' I said.

'I know,' said Mum as she stroked my hair.

I'm not giving up easily. I'm going to do something to help Tara.

I just have to figure out what.

I immediately emailed Leo and Anita, my fellow Adventure Club members, who I went to Nepal with, to see what they thought. A few minutes later, the phone rang.

On the sofa, a few minutes later

It was Leo on the phone.

'We **HAVE** to do something to help find Tara,' he said.

'I know!' I replied. 'But what?'

There was a pause.

'What did Julia say?' asked Leo.

My heart leapt. 'Of course! Julia will know what to do. Great idea, Leo.'

Julia's the leader of the Adventure Club. I messaged her straight away. Mum said that it was actually Julia who helped her find Tara the cub for my birthday present in the first place so maybe she'll know where she is! If I have to wait for her reply much longer I might explode!

My bedroom, that evening

The phone hasn't stopped ringing all day!

After Leo, Anita rang. She said that finding Tara the tiger cub and her mum sounded like a job for the Adventure Club! I told her I'd already messaged Julia.

Then Julia rang.

'Hi Tilly,' she said. 'I recently ordered motion sensor cameras that capture photographs of wildlife for our next project, but we won't need them for a while. We could see if we could ship them out to the tiger reserve. They could set them up in the jungle and hopefully get a picture of the tigers.'

'That sounds **BRILLIANT!**' I replied.

'Good. I'll speak to the tiger reserve and see what they think.'

After a while, Julia rang me back.

'The tiger reserve said that it's definitely worth a try, but they're short staffed. I'm going to see if I can go out there. Hopefully Steve can join me too.'

Steve was the Adventure Club vet. I beamed, pleased that the tigers were going to get some help. And then, without thinking, I said, 'Can Leo, Anita and I come too? We could be LOADS of help.'

There was a pause.

I crossed my fingers. And I tried to cross my toes.

'Well ... we could definitely do with extra help,' said Julia. 'Let me talk to your parents.'

My jaw dropped. I never expected her to **ACTUALLY** say yes (or at least maybe). This means we might get the Adventure Club back together much sooner than planned!

HOORAY!

(Although Mum is giving me a look that says don't get too excited yet.)

The Second Adventure

> **Objective:** Reunite the Adventure Club.

> **Obstacles:** Our parents! And the fact that India is really, really far away.

Home, two days later

I have the **BEST** news.

Julia and Steve have decided to make finding Tara the tiger cub the next Adventure Club project. And even better ... Leo, Anita and I get to go with them! Our mums and dads have all said yes!

'Are you sure you want to go away again so soon?' Dad had asked when the email from Julia came through. 'I've only just got back from my work trip.' He ruffled my hair. 'I thought we could spend some time at home together. We could watch films, play board games, go swimming.'

'That all sounds really fun, Dad – but there's a tiger who needs my help!' I said. 'Do you think you could manage without me for five days?'

'It's going to be hard,' said Dad, 'but I'll try my very best.'

I tried to pack my bag but I wasn't too sure what I'd need in the jungle.

The Third Adventure

   Objective: To pack my adventure kit.

   Obstacles: Not knowing what to pack. Also, Marigold the cat is being difficult!

As soon as I opened my suitcase, Marigold leapt off the bed straight into it, then glared at me.

'Oh Marigold!' I said. 'I'm sorry I can't take you with me.'

She rolled on to her back in response and showed me her furry ginger tummy, trying to convince me to bring her with her cuteness.

Mum stuck her head around the door. 'I thought you could have a tiger patch on your shirt this time,' she said, showing me a tiny fabric tiger head. 'I got one for Leo and Anita too. I just spoke to their parents and they're going to drive or get the train here tomorrow to discuss things a bit more. It turns out our house is halfway between theirs.'

'**PERFECT!**' I said. 'We can all figure out what to pack together.' It had been three whole months since we've seen each other. I couldn't wait to see them.

To celebrate all the **BRILLIANT** news, I did a dance around the house. Dad joined in, then Mum too, and we did a conga line around the kitchen.

Home, the next evening

I'm sitting on my bed with my half packed suitcase next to me. Marigold is now lying on top of the bag rather than in it. I'm yawning because it has been a **BUSY** day, but I think I'm almost ready to go and help find Tara the tiger cub! We leave in three days' time!

When the doorbell rang this morning, I jumped up as quickly as a frog.

'I'll get it!' I shouted and dashed down the stairs. Mum and Dad had been preparing all morning making food, researching the tiger reserve and writing lists. It felt almost like a party!

I opened the door and Anita and Leo stood on the doorstep with their parents. One of Leo's dads wore a T-shirt with a tiger on it! Anita's mum smiled and rubbed her tummy – she was going to have a baby soon.

'Tilly!' shouted Leo and Anita, both opening their arms wide. We had a group hug.

'I'm so glad the Adventure Club is back together again!' said Anita.

But we couldn't celebrate just yet. We still had a tiger to find.

'Can you believe they're going off again?' asked Leo's dad.

'I feel like they only just came back!' said Mum.

'You can't stop when there are animals to help and adventures to be had!' I said and smiled at them.

The grown-ups went into the kitchen and we went upstairs to my room with snacks. I told Leo and Anita that I didn't know what to pack.

'Don't worry,' said Anita. 'I have a checklist.'
Anita is always very prepared.

'We're only going to have five days to find Tara
the cub and her mum. That's not very long,' said
Leo. 'Do you think we'll find them?'

'We have to,' I replied. 'We have to make sure
Tara the tiger cub is safe and has water.'

'I guess. Do you think we'll be safe out in the
jungle with all the big animals?' asked Leo. 'Dad
gave me a whistle to wear around my neck in case I
get lost.'

'It's the mosquitoes that I'm worried about,'
said Anita. 'My dad calls them blood suckers.' She
pulled a pretend-horrified face, but Leo looked
really scared.

'Don't worry,' I said. 'We can take bug spray!
And at least it'll be warm this time,' I added to

Anita. She hated the cold. 'Anita, can I see your packing list?' I asked.

She nodded and handed it to me. It said:

Clothes – it'll be HOT!
Hiking boots ✓
MOSQUITO REPELLENT ✓
Water bottle ✓
Sun hat ✓
Sunglasses ✓
Head torch ✓
Lip balm ✓
Sun cream ✓
Swimming costume ✓

I put all of those things in my bag and added my toy cat, Poppy. She came with me on my last

Adventure Club trip. I couldn't leave her behind this time.

By the time Anita and Leo had to leave, Mum had sewn the tiger patches on to our adventure outfits and I'd finished packing. All that's left to do now is **WAIT!** I'll see Anita and Leo at the airport in three days, but it feels like it's three **YEARS** away! If only I could speed time up.

Ms Perry isn't going to believe it when she reads my adventure notebook!

Three days later, at the airport

The Fourth Adventure

> **Objective:** Travel to India
>
> **Obstacles:** Saying goodbye to Marigold my cat, Mum and Dad. And the biggest obstacle of all – a broken clock!

I'm sitting on the plane out of breath because I had to **RUN** through the airport to make it on to the plane in time.

Our kitchen clock stopped working at exactly 11.57am and we needed to leave by 12.30pm. It took us a whole hour to realise that the clock had stopped, so by then we were late!

'What a day for our clock to stop,' said Dad, once we were in the car. He wiped his forehead.

And then we hit traffic.

That slowed us down even more.

I was **EXTREMELY** worried the whole drive. 'Are you sure you can't go a teeny bit faster?'

Dad shook his head. I folded my arms.

'We've still got time,' said Mum, tight lipped and worried.

Once we arrived, we all ran through the airport together, weaving in and out of people and their suitcases.

I spotted Julia, the Adventure Club leader, and Steve the vet by the security gate, looking around anxiously. I ran over and hugged them. I hardly had any time to say goodbye to Mum and Dad (that part was sad) before I was whisked away on a special electric shuttle cart through the airport because I was sooooo late (that part was pretty cool).

'Thank you for saving Tara the tiger,' I said to Julia, as we sped through the airport.

'Don't thank us yet,' said Julia. 'You know there's still a chance we might not be able to find her.'

'I know,' I said.

That wasn't actually true. I am absolutely **ONE**

HUNDRED PER CENT certain that we'll find Tara the tiger cub safe and sound.

Thirteen hours later, the Adventure Club jet

In India, we switched from our big plane to the colourful Adventure Club jet that would take us to our final destination: a small airport in south-west India. It was a **TINY** plane that could only fit ten people inside. We had travelled on it for the first Adventure Club trip too! The walls were painted with pictures of different landscapes and the animals in them. I was sitting next to a picture of a waterfall with colourful birds flying through the air.

My stomach growled. I'd slept the whole journey to India which meant I'd missed all the meals and I was **STARVING**.

'What's this?' asked Leo, turning over a card that he'd found in the seat pocket.

I reached into the seat pocket in front of me and pulled out the same square card. It was a menu! Thank goodness!

Adventure Jet Menu

Red panda pretzels

Llama lemonade

Flamingo fizz

Sloth sandwich

Parrot popcorn

Cheetah chocolate

Python pizza

'Yum!' said Leo, smacking his lips together.

'I'm going to try the llama lemonade,' said Anita.

'I want to try **EVERYTHING!**' I said.

Now I'm veryyyyy full and the jet's about to land!
Yippeeee!

Day one, India
A café in the airport, early morning

The Fifth Adventure

> **Objective:** Getting to the tiger reserve.
> **Obstacles:** Everyone else taking ages to get ready!

It's been thirty minutes since we landed and we're waiting in a café for Steve to finish getting supplies before we're taken to the tiger reserve. As you know, I find waiting a big **CHALLENGE** but I'm trying to be patient. I'm writing in my notebook to distract myself from thinking about Tara the tiger cub!

Just when Steve was finally ready, Anita said she had to

go to the bathroom, and then Leo said that he wanted a snack! I rolled my eyes. This was taking for ever!

Three hours later, in the jeep on the way to the Big Tiger Reserve

When everyone was finally ready to go, Julia and Steve led us outside to the parked jeep.

A rush of heat and stickiness hit me as soon as we stepped outside. The sun was low in the sky, which was hazy and orange.

'It's hot!' said Anita happily behind me. She skipped along the road.

Anita smelled lemony and minty from her mosquito repellent.

'There's the jeep!' said Steve, pointing at an olive-green jeep.

'Who's driving us there?' asked Leo, looking around.

'I am!' said Steve. 'Everyone in!'

Julia loaded the wildlife cameras into the boot and we piled into the back and drove off with the windows down.

In town, it was loud, with beeping cars, winding motorbikes and music from open-fronted shops. The shops were selling all different kinds of things – vegetables, flowers, shoes … one just had loads and loads of sparkly bangles! I'm going to ask Julia if I can get some for Mum on the way home.

We stopped in traffic next to a street market stall selling baskets full of bright red, yellow and orange spices. Even though I was still full from the plane, the smell of the spices and the street food being cooked across the road made my stomach start to grumble again. Two cows with curly horns pulling a cart walked past us.

'Can we go in one of them?' asked Leo, pointing at it.

'Only if you don't want to arrive until tomorrow,' said Steve with a smile.

'What about on a motorbike?' Leo suggested as one zoomed by.

Steve laughed and shook his head.

'What about a rickshaw?' I asked as a bright yellow-and-black, three-wheeled rickshaw sped past.

'Are you lot trying to say something about my driving?' said Steve, laughing.

Once we were out of town there was less traffic and more people riding bicycles. Green forests and long flooded rows of flat land for growing rice, called paddy fields, stretched into the distance. For a few minutes we had to wait because a cow had laid down in the middle of the road! But we were right by a roadside stall selling coconuts and watermelons, so we got a snack, and waiting for the cow to move again wasn't too bad.

After about forty-five minutes the road turned into a dirt track and the landscape became hilly. The undergrowth of grasses beneath the trees were dry and yellow.

'The forest here smells different to the woods at home,' I said.

'It's the protected sandalwood and teak trees,' replied Steve. 'They have a very distinct scent.'

We jolted over a bump in the road and the jeep slowed.

I saw flashes of blue and green feathers in the road ahead.

'Look,' I whispered, pointing.

'A peacock!' said Leo.

It opened its long feathers into a fan and danced, shimmying in a circle.

'Mum dances like that when she cleans the kitchen to music,' I said. 'She shakes her shoulders.' And I imitated her.

We slowly drove around the peacock.

'We're almost there!' said Julia.

As we continued driving my stomach started to turn over uncomfortably. It might have been because of the winding roads but I think it was also because I was nervous about how huge the task ahead of us was.

I knew that the tiger reserve was the same size as the whole of the city of London. Dad had said that finding Tara the tiger cub would be like finding a needle in a haystack. I hadn't really understood what he meant until I watched the endless jungle speed past me. I cupped my head in my hands. It seemed like an impossible task.

We're just pulling into the tiger reserve, which will become our Adventure Club HQ for the next five days, so I'd better go and help unpack the jeep.

Adventure Club HQ, mid-morning
I'm sitting in front of a fan on the veranda. Now that the sun's fully up, it's hotter than the time we went to the beach during a heatwave. It's hotter than the time I accidentally ate a chilli pepper! It's **SO** hot that all I want is a cold shower.

When we first arrived, Julia gathered us all outside the building. 'We have a surprise for you,' she said. 'Rhyah and Adi have said that we can stay here at the orphaned elephant calf sanctuary that's part of the tiger reserve.'

My mouth dropped open. If you'd have been able to see my face, it would have looked like this ...

'You mean we're staying in the same place the baby elephants stay?' asked Leo.

'There are elephant calves here **RIGHT NOW?**' asked Anita.

'Yes,' said Steve, nodding enthusiastically. 'You might even get the chance to feed one,' he whispered.

Anita, Leo and I all beamed at each other.

'Here they are now,' said Julia suddenly.

I turned my head around, expecting to see the elephants, but it was the wildlife managers, Rhyah and Adi.

'Welcome!' said Rhyah. She had long hair, plaited and twisted up on the top of her head, friendly eyes and a small gap between her front teeth when she smiled. She looked like this ...

'It's great to meet you all,' said Adi. 'Come inside,' He had short black hair, a big smile and was wearing sunglasses.

He looked like this ...

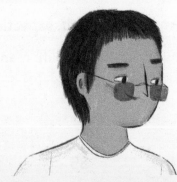

'This will be our Adventure Club HQ meeting room,' said Julia, as we followed Adi and Rhyah on to a huge covered veranda enclosed by screens.

Wicker and rope chairs hung from the ceiling. On the back wall by the door a mosaic of shiny pottery formed the shapes of a tiger and an elephant.

We all jumped on to the swinging chairs. I kicked my legs back and forth.

Rhyah stood up in front of us. 'There are lots of different animals that live in the tiger reserve here – not just tigers. But Adi and I are on the tiger team. I'm in charge of the tigers' safety.'

'And I'm in charge of monitoring them,' chimed in Adi.

'We're very happy you're here to help,' said Rhyah. 'Because of the late monsoon, the rest of our team are away helping the other animals that need water. There are also more poachers around.

We'll need you to help us with the orphaned elephants here too as the elephant team are away helping a herd that was targeted by poachers.'

Anita gasped. 'Elephants are my favourite animals!' she whispered to me.

'There's no time to lose so we're going to start right away,' said Adi. 'Our job today will be to place the cameras. That way we'll hopefully be able to find Tara the tiger cub.'

'Julia and I will check that none of the cameras got damaged on the journey here,' said Steve.

'And before we go, we need to talk about safety,' said Rhyah. 'This is a wild area, so there are some rules to follow. We have a checklist for each time we go into the jungle.' She was holding up a big sign. It said:

→ Check your shoes to make sure no insect has decided to make them its home for the night.

→ Fill up your water bottle with filtered water.

→ Remember your day bag, sun hat and sunscreen.

→ Make sure you tell us if you feel at all unwell. It's easy to get dehydrated.

→ Remember that the animals here are wild. We don't touch them. Try to leave them as undisturbed as possible. We don't want them to get used to humans as then they could be poached more easily.

I nodded. This was serious and important. I didn't want to get it wrong.

Anita wrote down the checklist in her own notebook. I copied it down here too, just in case. Leo was already checking his shoes for insects. (I imagined a spider hanging out in his shoe and having a party.)

'Can we ride an elephant?' asked Leo as he put his shoe back on.

'They're an endangered species so we feel it's wrong to tame them to be ridden,' explained Rhyah gently. 'We need to focus all our attention here on making sure the ones in the wild are safe and that we can send any that get hurt back out into the wild.'

'OK.' Leo nodded.

'Do you have any questions?' asked Adi.

'I do,' said Leo. 'How will the cameras know that the tigers are there?'

'That's a good question, Leo!' said Rhyah. 'The cameras that you brought with you have an infrared beam. It's invisible but when the tigers walk past it the camera goes off and captures photographs of them.'

'And how do we know where to put the cameras?' I asked.

Adi sighed. 'That's the tricky bit. Hopefully we'll find a paw print or someone will have spotted one that will tell us which area they're in. And then we can put the cameras you've brought around that area.'

'We'll leave water out for them too. Hopefully that will entice them,' added Rhyah.

Adi knelt and set up a projector screen on the back wall as Julia and Steve unpacked and checked the cameras.

'You can test the cameras out yourselves,' said Steve. 'I've set one up over there.' He pointed to the other end of the room.

We ran over and waved our arms over the invisible sensor, setting off the camera.

Then Adi showed us the pictures. He said that I could keep these ones.

The cameras worked so well that I started to feel much more confident that we were going to find Tara the tiger cub and her mum than I had been earlier.

'Where are the elephants now?' asked Anita.

'I'll show you,' said Adi. 'We've just got time for a quick tour before we go.'

Adi showed us the vet clinic and examination room, the outdoor paddock and the animal ambulance (which was painted with pictures of elephants!).

'The ambulance is how we rescue any hurt or stranded animals. And how we take them back to the wild when they're ready to be released,' said Adi.

I wondered if any animals would need to be rescued while we were here.

'Follow me,' said Adi, continuing the tour. He led us up a staircase on the outside of the building to the rooftop. There was a whole rooftop hangout with cushions, plants and a wicker bench! The view of the jungle was **AMAZING!**

Next, we saw the elephant nursery.

'We're currently hand-rearing two orphaned elephants. In a few years, once they're old enough to survive on their own, they'll be rehabilitated back to the wild.'

Adi pointed at a window and inside were two elephant calves.

Anita squealed at the sight of them.

'Meet Mishka and Mo. Mo is a tiny bit bigger than Mishka. That's how you can tell them apart,' said Adi.

Mo was trotting around the room, his head gently bobbing up and down as he ran. He kept treading on his own trunk.

Mishka was lying down on her side, looking like

she was ready to sleep. She flapped her ear and tucked her feet up in front of her. With her long eyelashes and wrinkly extra layers of skin, she reminded me a bit of my neighbour's pug puppy.

'Notice their ears,' says Adi. 'I think they look as if they're shaped like the Indian subcontinent.'

I nodded, even though I didn't really know what shape the Indian subcontinent was. I asked Julia later and she said it's like this:

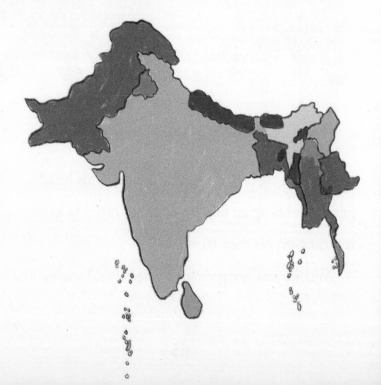

'Can we feed them?' asked Leo hopefully.

'Please?' added Anita. 'Pretty, pretty please?'

Adi laughed. 'In the morning you can. First we've got important tiger-finding work to do. Why don't you all rest on the veranda while we prepare a few things for our journey?'

So that's where I've been. But Rhyah has just come running up to say that she has important news about the tigers so I have to go!

Update, a few minutes later

Rhyah said that she'd just been told of a possible sighting of Tara the tiger cub and her mum near one of the villages on the outskirts of the reserve.

'It's good that they're close to a village, right?' I said, thinking that there must be water in a village.

'Actually, it's bad,' Rhyah said. 'We try to limit

human and tiger contact as it creates conflict. The tigers might attack someone if they're hungry or eat their livestock. Or poachers might hear they're close by and try to get them.'

'Oh no!' said Leo.

'But the good thing is that now we can set up the cameras there to see if it's really them and if they're OK,' said Adi.

Rhyah nodded, looking excited. 'Now that we know where to set the cameras up, I think we've got a really good chance of finding them.'

'What happens when we find them?' I asked.

'We'll bring them water, and then if they're still heading out of the reserve, we'll have to catch them and bring them back,' said Rhyah.

'And then they'll be safe?' asked Leo.

'As long as they stay within the protected area. The problem is, if it doesn't rain soon, they may leave to go searching for a bigger water source again. That's where their prey – the food they eat – will be,' said Rhyah.

I looked up at the sky. It was completely clear and blue. I sighed. There was no sign of rain.

Rhyah knows **ALL** about tigers. I want to be just like her when I'm older.

The jeep, a bit later

The Sixth Adventure

    Objective: Travel to the village.

    Obstacles: The jungle between us.

I skipped alongside Julia as we fetched our day bags and the camera equipment.

We all piled into an open-topped jeep, the front painted in orange and black tiger camouflage stripes and the back in leopard spots.

'I wish my car at home was like this,' said Leo.

'You'd get really wet when it rained though!' I replied.

'And cold in winter,' added Anita, shivering even though it was super warm.

I put on my sun hat to protect myself from the hot sun. Even under the shade from the tree canopy, I could feel it piercing my skin. The jeep rolled over the dirt tracks through the jungle.

'If the jeep slows down, make sure to stay very still and quiet. It could be because we've spotted wildlife,' said Steve.

'Everyone duck!' said Julia, as we passed underneath some low hanging vines.

A minute later the jeep slowed and Anita, Leo

and I looked at each other excitedly. Could it be an animal? A tiger?

Julia handed me her binoculars. 'Look,' she said softly, 'over there.'

I raised them to my eyes and focused. In the small circle was a four-horned antelope grazing on the dry grasses.

Leo got so excited when it was his turn to look that he wriggled in his seat, almost tipping over the side.

'Hang on!' said Steve, steadying Leo. 'Remember, hands and legs inside.'

The animal leapt away and the jeep continued onward. Then a second later it stopped abruptly.

'You don't need binoculars for this one,' said Julia. 'Look!'

Ahead of us was a whole **HERD** of elephants marching through the trees. The herd was made up of elephants of all sizes and the smallest two were trotting alongside their mothers at the back. They were even smaller than Mishka and Mo! Every now and then, the herd stopped to let them catch up.

'This herd is led by their great-grandma,' Adi told us, pointing to the extra-large elephant at the front with wrinkly ear flaps.

I felt so **LUCKY** to be able to see them. I wanted to do everything I could to protect these amazing animals.

All of a sudden, as I was watching the two calves through the binoculars to get an even closer look, **DISASTER** struck! The smallest one, who was last in line, slipped down a ditch.

'Where's the other calf?' asked Anita.

'It hasn't got back up the slope,' I said.

'Oh no!' said Leo. 'The herd's moving away. They don't realise!'

Rhyah radioed back to the team at the tiger reserve to send the ambulance **AS SOON AS POSSIBLE.**

We sat down and waited but the herd was getting further and further away. They were moving so quickly.

'Unless we get the elephant calf back soon, it might never be able to go back to its herd,' said Steve.

Just then the animal ambulance **FINALLY** arrived. The huge van raced up the dirt track in a cloud of dust. Rhyah flagged it down and pointed to where the calf was stuck. The ambulance rolled to a stop ahead of us and two people I didn't recognise jumped out. Steve ran up to help them and they all climbed down into the ditch to examine the elephant.

We had to stay back in the jeep and watch. I bit my nails as we waited.

'It's taking a long time,' said Anita. 'I hope the elephant calf isn't hurt.'

Just then, Rhyah and Steve scrambled out of the ditch and the elephant calf was passed up to them. They placed the calf in the ambulance. The doors shut and Rhyah turned and gave us a thumbs up. That meant that the calf wasn't injured. Phew!

After transporting the calf as close to the herd as was safe, they released it. We followed along in the jeep and waited anxiously.

The elephant calf bounded towards them and the herd welcomed her back happily.

'How lovely,' Julia said as we watched them reunite.

'It's brilliant!' I said.

I'm already worried about Tara. I'm glad that I don't have to worry about another baby animal!

Now we're off again, speeding towards the village where Tara and her mum were spotted. We're sitting in the open back of the jeep, which is amazing! But the road is so bumpy that I can hardly read my own writing. I'm going to have to tell you about the rest of the day later!

The veranda, after dinner

The rest of the trip was **VERY BUSY!** The village was a collection of mud brick houses nestled beneath the hills. Cows, buffalo and birds dotted the fields around it. A family was waiting for us on the road when we arrived. They were eager to tell us what happened. Adi translated everything they said into English so that we could understand.

'I was hanging up the washing when I saw a tiger with a cub leap over the wall just outside the house!' a young woman said excitedly. 'I shouted to everyone else and we watched as they crossed the road and headed in that direction.' She pointed to the right.

'Luckily they didn't come too close,' said the mum.

'Or try and eat the goats,' added the dad.

'That must have been scary,' said Julia.

'Over there is where we'll set up the cameras,' said Rhyah. 'Thank you for your help.'

We waved goodbye and headed into the jungle.

'I hope that they're still in this area,' I said, crossing my fingers for luck.

> **The Seventh Adventure:**
>
> **Objective:** To set up the motion sensor cameras.
>
> **Obstacles:** Finding the perfect spot. Disguising the cameras.

Rhyah and Adi began setting up the cameras.

'For the best chance of getting photographs of the tigers, we have to disguise the cameras by camouflaging them to look like the environment,' said Rhyah, as she balanced a camera on a rock.

'Tigers are very inquisitive,' said Adi. 'If they find the cameras they might try and play with them and break them.'

'We'll cover them in leaves and twigs so that they don't stand out,' said Rhyah.

'But be careful when you pick up the sticks and anything off the ground. We don't want to disturb any creepy crawlies!' said Julia.

'Do you get scorpions here?' asked Leo.

'Yes, definitely,' replied Rhyah.

'I'll let you turn over all the rocks then,' Leo said, grimacing. Leo had found a scorpion in his tent when we were staying in Nepal and he had **NOT** been happy about it.

'Not a bad idea. In fact, it's probably best to wait for me or Adi before you touch anything,' said Rhyah.

Soon we were searching for the best spots for the cameras. I noticed a **HUGE** pile of leaves. It was the **PERFECT** place to hide a camera! I headed towards it and reached out to grab a handful—

'What are you doing?' asked Anita. 'We're supposed to wait for Rhyah or Adi before we touch anything.'

'Rhyah?' I called. 'I think I've found a good spot

for one of the cameras!'

'Just a minute, Tilly,' Rhyah called.

I tapped my foot and waited. After a minute, (it must have been at least a minute because it felt like ages) I looked back at Rhyah. She was by the jeep, assembling a tripod with Adi. Steve, Julia and Leo were watching a bird and facing the other direction.

I'd had enough of waiting for people. Tara the tiger cub needed my help urgently. And this spot was absolutely perfect for a camera. I was sure that Rhyah would think so too.

'I'll be really careful,' I said, reaching for a handful of leaves.

'Tilly, are you sure we shouldn't wait?' said Anita, crouching down a few feet behind me.

'Stop!' shouted Rhyah.

I froze.

'What's wrong?' I whispered. My heart raced.

'Come away from there,' said Rhyah. Her voice was quiet but sharp and urgent.

I knew instantly that something was wrong.

I backed away from the leaves towards the rest of the group and turned to face everyone. Anita and Leo were staring at me with wide eyes and worried expressions.

'Let's keep moving,' said Rhyah softly. 'That's a snake's nest. It would have been very dangerous if you'd disturbed it.'

It turned out that it wasn't just any snake's nest. It was a **KING COBRA'S** nest. King cobras are the snakes that have a hood and look like this.

They can spit deadly venom, which is terrifying but also a little bit awesome.

I have **NEVER** moved so fast, getting far away from the nest. I pictured the snake's forked tongue flicking. A nest meant there was a mother around somewhere too.

'They're the only snakes to build nests like that,' said Adi. 'Oh, and did I mention that they eat other snakes!'

'Ew!' said Anita.

'Oh no!' said Leo, hurrying even farther away. 'That's awful!'

I didn't say anything. All I could think was that if I'd been bitten by a snake I could have ruined everything! Everyone would then have been focusing on me instead of Tara the tiger cub. Why couldn't I be more patient? It was **NOT** good. I sighed loudly.

I glanced back at the snake's nest. Adi noticed and smiled sympathetically at me.

'Don't worry,' he said, 'we'll find somewhere good to set up the cameras.'

'That was quite a close call you had,' said Rhyah, walking next to me. 'Are you feeling OK?'

'I care about Tara the tiger so much and I wanted to show everyone that I can help ... but I did the opposite. I wish I could be like you,' I said.

'Don't be too hard on yourself, Tilly,' said Rhyah. 'I've had years of training. You've already done so much to be proud of in your effort to find Tara the tiger cub. We just have to make sure that we're all safe out here in the jungle too.'

I nodded and felt a bit better. 'I just hope we find Tara and her mum soon,' I said.

'Me too,' said Rhyah.

Adi spotted a path of flattened grass ahead.

'This could be a path that's used by the tigers. Let's put a camera here. You can pick up those rocks and twigs over there.'

'Help me set up this one, Tilly,' said Leo.

We covered the camera with rocks and twigs and after that it was easier to find other spots.

We set up five cameras in total. This is where we put them.

1. Near the flattened grass.
2. Beside a tiny puddle that's usually a small river (I hope they find it because then they'll have something to drink).
3. Behind some rocks.
4. On a path between thick bushes.
5. Under leaves (that weren't part of the snake's nest!).

Just as we were putting up the last of the cameras, we spotted some grey monkeys moving

through the trees above us. We all
stopped to watch them.

There was a trickle of water
from above.

'I think the monkey weed on me!'
said Anita, touching her wet arm.

Me and Leo got the giggles.

'It's not funny. It got on my hair,' said Anita.

Leo and I still couldn't stop laughing. Julia got
out some wet wipes. 'You'll be dry again in just a
second. You can be the first one to have a shower
when we get back to the sanctuary.'

Anita glared at us.

But then a baby monkey swung through the branches towards its mum, grabbed on to her fur, and peeked out at us. It made a squeaking sound and even Anita smiled a bit.

'Come on,' said Julia. 'Let's get you all back to the tiger reserve.'

'Now we just have to wait for the next twelve hours and then Rhyah and I will go back to get the cameras and see if they've captured anything,' said Adi.

Twelve hours! I didn't know how I'd be able to wait that long. I wanted to check them straight away!

Just as we were getting ready to leave, there was a barking sound. Rhyah put her hand out for us to stop and be still. 'That's the deer's warning call,' she said excitedly. 'It means there might be a tiger around.'

'We have to get back to the jeep, quickly now,' said Julia.

The Eighth Adventure

Objective: Get back to the jeep safely.

Obstacles: There could be a tiger around!

(Hopefully it's Tara the tiger cub and her mum.)

We moved quickly through the grassy forest. Twigs cracked under my feet. Birds scattered from the trees around us. I searched around me, hoping for a glimpse of Tara the cub, but I didn't see anything and then before I knew it we were in the jeep heading back to the reserve.

When we finally made it back, Adi asked if we wanted dinner. By that time my stomach was rumbling loudly. I was **STARVING**. I was also feeling very tired and a bit wobbly ... what if we don't get a photograph of Tara the tiger cub in the next twelve hours?

For a starter Rhyah brought us whole coconuts and a paper straw, which made me forget about feeling worried for a bit. We drank the water out of the middle before cutting the coconut open and eating the flesh. It was delicious.

Then we had lentils and rice and a masala dosa, which is the coolest thing to eat ever! It's like a giant, thin, crispy, pancake that's rolled up. It's so long that it could fit on two plates!

'This is important tiger-finding fuel,' said Julia. 'You'll need it for tomorrow.'

Inside the mosquito net, that night

I couldn't wait to find out where we were going to be sleeping. In the first Adventure Club trip we slept in tents in the mountains.

'Maybe we'll be on the roof under the stars,' said Anita excitedly.

'Or maybe we'll be so close to the elephants we'll be able to hear them snoring!' said Leo.

But it turned out we were sleeping in a boring room with bunk beds and mosquito nets. There was nothing else inside.

Still, there were elephants nearby and hopefully tigers too, and **THAT** was pretty exciting.

'Which bed do you think will be safest?' asked Leo. 'And most likely to be away from the creepy crawlies?'

'You have your mosquito net,' said Julia, reassuring him. 'That should keep everything out.'

'It was amazing watching that elephant calf re-join its herd,' said Leo as we clambered into bed. 'I wish we could be here to watch Mo and Mishka go back out into the wild.'

'Me too,' I replied. 'That probably won't be for a few years though.'

'Hey, I'm trying to get some sleep over here,' said Anita.

I feel all cosy in my silk sleeping bag, surrounded by my mosquito net. There are huge fans that whir around on the ceiling. Cicadas buzz outside. I hug Poppy my toy cat.

'Goodnight Leo. Goodnight Anita,' I say.

'Goodnight, Tilly!' they reply.

I'm so nervous about tomorrow and seeing the photographs. I hope with **ALL** my might that there will be a photo of Tara.

Day two, the elephant paddock, morning

After breakfast this morning we got to help take care of the elephants, but I couldn't concentrate – even though the calves were **VERY** cute. I kept remembering how I'd almost ruined everything yesterday with the snake. I felt anxious to find Tara and make it all better. I just wanted to look at the pictures!

'Are the photographs ready?' I asked Adi.

'Not yet,' he replied. 'Rhyah's just left to go and retrieve the memory cards with the photographs on them from the cameras.'

After a few minutes, I walked up to him again.

'How about now?' I asked.

'How about I come and find you the moment Rhyah's back? Does that sound good?' Adi replied, smiling.

'That sounds great,' I said and high-fived him.

'She'll be an hour or two still,' said Adi. 'And in the meantime, the elephants really need a bath.'

The Ninth Adventure

Objective: Give the elephants a bath.

Obstacles: Elephants don't like to stay still and they think bath time is a game!

Outside the paddock, Adi and Julia handed Anita and Leo hoses before they started sweeping and tidying next to us. I didn't feel like joining in, so I watched from a bench by the main building while they sprayed water on Mishka and Mo.

Anita held the hose up so that it trickled down over Mishka's back and Mishka moved her trunk through it, playing, before attempting to take the hose out of Anita's hand. Anita couldn't stop laughing. It was pretty cute, but I was still feeling too worried about Tara to laugh.

Anita put her hose down and walked up to me. 'Come and join us,' she said. 'Why are you sitting over here?'

'I'm just thinking about Tara. I should have listened to you yesterday when you said to wait before touching those leaves – I almost ruined everything,' I said.

'But you didn't!' she replied. 'We still have loads to learn about this place, that's all. I didn't know there were snakes there either, I was just trying to follow the rules. They told us to wait for our own safety.'

'I'll try to be more patient from now on,' I said with a sigh.

'You can start now!' said Leo jokingly, hearing the end of our conversation. 'Come and play with the elephants. It will make the time go faster, I promise. And you'll be helping too.'

They each grabbed one of my hands and pulled me up.

'OK,' I said, laughing. 'I suppose I could help.'

Julia and Adi watched as we finished bathing the elephants.

The calves ran up and down alongside the paddock fence before rolling in the mud. Then Mo sucked up water with his trunk and blew it back out at us, spraying it **EVERYWHERE**. He clearly thought that we needed a bath too! We all laughed and shrieked.

'Oh dear,' said Julia, but she was smiling.

By the time we had finished we were **COVERED** in mud.

After the bath it was time to feed the elephants **GIANT** bottles of milk. We took it in turns to feed them. Adi and Rhyah told me all about Asian elephants.

Things that I've learnt so far:

- An elephant's trunk is a long nose. They use it for breathing, smelling, trumpeting, and as a tool to gather water and grab things. They have no bones in their trunk.
- The folds in their skin can hold water.
- There are differences between Asian elephants and African elephants. For example, African elephants have much larger ears.
- Some male Asian elephants start growing tusks when they're about two years old. Their tusks are actually teeth.
- Dust and mud baths keep their skin cool and protected from sunburn.
- They eat all the time. (About twelve to eighteen hours a day.)
- They can hold the tips of their trunks above water and snorkel!

Now I'm writing in my notebook as Leo and Anita take their turn to feed Mishka and Mo. Leo and Anita have **HUMONGOUS** smiles planted on their faces. They look like this:

The veranda, after lunch

FINALLY, when we were finishing our lunch and I was beginning to think the photos would **NEVER** be ready, Adi came running up to tell us it was time.

I bit my nails, hoping with all my might that there would be a photo of Tara the tiger cub. We sat down in a circle on the veranda with Julia and Steve, Adi and Rhyah.

'Lots of animals came and sniffed the cameras,' said Adi. 'Look!'

He passed us a photograph of an animal he said was a striped neck mongoose. It looked like a startled, dark-haired meerkat to me.

Then there was one of a **HUGE** bison with gigantic horns that Rhyah said was called a gaur.

I gasped at the next one.

A leopard slinking past, its beautiful green eyes alert and focused.

Then there was an antelope, a porcupine with its quills up, and a small green bird which Rhyah said was a white-cheeked barbet.

'My favourite picture is of this gaur,' said Leo. 'It looks as if he's taking a selfie.'

'But was there a tiger?' I asked quietly. My stomach turned nervously.

There was a sparkle in her eye as Rhyah handed us the last photograph.

There, caught by the camera, trying to drink from dried-up river, was Tara the tiger cub and her mother. Her head was lowered, drinking from the last droplets of water. Because I'd looked at pictures of her so often back home, I could recognise her by her stripes.

I let out a huge sigh of relief. Now we knew
that they were safe and alive and together.

But Rhyah still looked worried.

'Isn't this good news?' I asked.

'It's good news we found them. And we know
they've had some water. But they're not safe
yet. From the direction they were travelling, it
seems like Tara and her mum are heading towards

another village.'

That meant that they were at risk of being killed by poachers! Or chased away and separated, or even caught in a trap.

'Oh no!' I said. 'How are we going to make sure that they're safe now?'

'It will be impossible for us to catch them out here as there are too many places they could be,' added Adi.

Everyone looked at each other with concerned expressions. We'd have to think of something, but it wouldn't be easy.

Bunk beds, bedtime
I don't think I'll be able to sleep even a wink tonight. I'm far too worried about Tara and her mum! Rhyah says that there is nothing we can do until tomorrow. But I wish there was something more that I could do

to help **NOW!** I'm hugging Poppy the cat and trying to be more patient, but this is worse than waiting for Christmas Day!

Day three, Adventure Club HQ veranda, early morning

You'll **NEVER** guess what just happened.

Julia woke us up a few minutes ago at dawn, which felt like the middle of the night! The sun was a big ball, low in the sky, and it was already warm, even though it wasn't properly light yet. We gathered for breakfast and there Rhyah announced that ... wait for it ... we were going to go in a helicopter to find Tara the tiger cub and her mum!

We'll get to use special thermal binoculars that mean that we can spot animals through the trees! And we can check for water sources too. Rhyah and Adi are still worried that they're not getting enough water and that's why they're heading towards the village.

We leave in three hours. I'm so happy I could sing, or dance. Maybe I'll do both — oh I'd better go. I think something's wrong with Anita, she's crying.

The bedroom
Anita wants to go home. She had a mosquito stuck inside her mosquito net last night and she didn't realise. Her bites have come up as big red blotches and they're **EVERYWHERE**.

'Even though I did everything right, I still got bitten by mosquitoes. It's not fair,' Anita said as Julia dabbed some cream on her bites.

Leo put his arm over her shoulder.

Anita sniffed and said, 'I'm not very good at being in the Adventure Club.'

'That's not true!' Leo and I both said, each holding her hand to help her feel better.

'You're doing brilliantly in the Adventure Club!' said Julia. 'It's OK to feel homesick, or sad, or scared. It doesn't mean that you're doing anything wrong, or that you're not part of the Adventure Club.'

'We're a team, remember,' added Steve.

'The Adventure Club Tiger Team!' I said.

Anita smiled and wiped her eyes. 'I really miss my baby brother and my dog Teddy though.'

'I wish we could do something to make Anita feel better,' Leo whispered to me when Anita had gone to brush her teeth. 'I don't want her to leave!'

I didn't want Anita to leave either so I put on my thinking hat (which was also my sun hat). There was still a bit of time before we were going to ride in the helicopter.

'I have an idea!' I said.

The Tenth Adventure

Objective: Cheer up Anita.

Obstacle: Not being at home – the one thing
she really wants.

Julia helped Anita speak to her mum on her
phone, even though it was the middle of the night
at home. While Anita was busy talking, we decided
to decorate our bedroom to make it more like an
Adventure Club den.

First we chased out any mosquitoes with a fan.
Then we got some chalk and drew all her favourite
things on the walls: elephants, dogs, stars and
rainbows. Rhyah gave me some old saris to drape
from the ceiling for colour and found some small

torches to use as fairy lights.

I stood back and nodded at our work. It looked brilliant.

The elephant paddock, one hour later
Anita loved the bedroom decorations. She smiled and said, 'I'm going to stay. I've decided.'

'Yes!' I said and high-fived her. It wouldn't feel like the Adventure Club without Anita here.

'Hooray!' said Leo. 'Was it my drawing of an elephant that convinced you to stay?'

We all laughed.

'We just have time to bathe the elephants before you go on the helicopter,' said Rhyah. 'Come on.'

The baby elephants were familiar with the morning routine and trumpeted and pranced alongside us as we walked alongside the fence.

As we reached the corner of the paddock with the hoses, I felt something itchy on my arm and looked down. There was a huge, hairy, green caterpillar, hanging out and treating my arm like a branch:

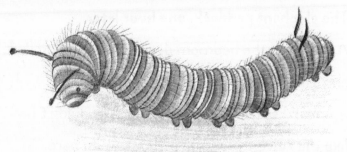

I jumped and the caterpillar went flying off my arm and landed on a tall blade of grass.

'Oh no!' I shouted. 'Is it OK?' I didn't hurt it, did I?'

'No, it's fine, look, it's walking off,' said Anita.

My skin was **EXTREMELY** itchy.

'I think it liked you so much it left you a present – some of its hairs,' said Rhyah.

'Are they poisonous hairs?' asked Leo. 'Is her

arm going to fall off?'

I felt panicked. I didn't want anything to stop me from being able to go on this helicopter ride.

Rhyah laughed. 'No, luckily they're not poisonous. Tilly's arm is going to be just fine! I will, however, have to tweezer out all of these hairs before the helicopter ride.'

'So ... I can still go on the helicopter?' I asked, holding my breath.

'Of course!' said Rhyah.

Phew!

I perched on a rock so that Rhyah could see my arm better. The elephants approached, clearly wondering what was going on. Mishka put her trunk up to my shoulder. I could feel her warm breath through the end of her trunk. Then she tried to give me a hug by wrapping her trunk around me. I giggled and rubbed the top of her trunk.

I tried to sit really still while Rhyah pulled out the hairs one by one. It's wasn't painful, just very, **VERY** itchy and even the elephant calves weren't distracting me. Anita and Leo fed the calves their gigantic bottles of milk.

'Your arm is really red,' said Anita, coming over to look after Mo had finished eating.

Afterwards there was just enough time for a shower to wash any last hairs away. (There was a frog in the shower with me, croaking. And a spotty lizard on the windowsill!)

The helicopter landing pad, afternoon

The Eleventh Adventure:

　　Objective: Finding Tara the tiger cub and water for the animals.

　　Obstacles: Searching a **HUGE** area!

We all had to wear special headsets to go in the helicopter. There was just enough room for the three of us and Julia to sit inside. My heartbeat quickened as we took off.

'I feel like a bird!' shouted Leo over the noise of the engine and the spinning rotor blades.

Soon we were high above the trees. My tummy filled with butterflies. I could see the hilly jungle landscape and the dry winding riverbeds. I squinted and concentrated. It was important to look out for water spots for the animals. It was harder than I expected to see anything through the trees.

We took it in turns to look through the thermal binoculars. They lit up when they sensed body heat, so that we could see any animals hidden by the cover of the trees.

'Over there! Look!' said Leo, pointing. He wasn't using the binoculars.

In a field to our left was a herd of elephants. Their shadows stretched long on the ground next to them, as if they were four times the size. It looked like this:

Then, as we flew over a clearing, I noticed a break in the trees. Right below us was a deep blue pool. Groups of deer, bison and elephants were gathered around the outside of it.

I looked at Julia excitedly. We had found water! It was the perfect place for Tara the tiger cub and her mum.

But we still didn't know exactly where Tara was or how we'd get her to this waterhole! I hoped she hadn't got into trouble near the village!

'We're going to fly low down now,' said Julia. 'To try and spot if Tara and her mum are here.'

The helicopter whirred and swooped down, hovering just above the trees. We circled the waterhole, searching through the binoculars, but there were no tigers nearby. Julia told the pilot to try a wider circle.

We circled round and round. It felt like we had been looking for hours and finding nothing.

Then, just when I'd almost given up hope, Anita squealed. It was her turn to look through the binoculars, and she had been looking out of the window directly below us. 'Is that what I think it is?' she asked, handing Julia the thermal binoculars and pointing.

'What is it?' I asked.

'Have a look,' said Julia, handing me the binoculars.

I held them up to my eyes and scanned the land below. Everything was dark grey except for the animals, which glowed a pale grey colour. I saw the outline of elephants, a monkey, two deer and then ... a big cat shape. And a smaller one too, next to it. It had to be them! It had to be Tara the tiger cub and her mum.

'They've made it past the village and they're heading towards the waterhole,' said Julia, excitedly. 'The waterhole is in a protected area. But they're not out of danger yet. There's still a busy road that they have to cross. Look.' She pointed out of the window and I could see a road that snaked between the trees. 'And then there's more unprotected land where they're at risk from poachers.'

'Oh no!' I said. In the helicopter, I hadn't realised how far we'd travelled from the waterhole, and how dangerous it could still be for Tara and her mum to make it there.

Back on the ground, we told Rhyah and Adi what we had seen.

'How will we know if the tigers make it to the waterhole safely?' asked Leo, worriedly.

'Yeah, they could be poached or die of thirst or hunger or get run over on their way there!' I said, imagining the worst.

'We can't leave without knowing that they got there,' Anita added. 'And we're meant to be going home the day after tomorrow!'

I felt the same. Now that we'd found Tara the tiger cub, there was no way that I could go home without knowing that she was safe.

'We'll go and set up some more of the cameras at the waterhole,' said Rhyah. 'Hopefully we'll see them safely there soon. Tigers can travel thirty miles in a day, and the waterhole is well within that distance.'

'We'll set up the cameras this afternoon,' said Adi.

'We can help!' I said enthusiastically.

Julia and Steve glanced at each other. 'It's too dangerous for us all to go to the waterhole because there are so many animals there,' said Julia.

'We'll be **EXTRA** careful,' I said.

'Please, please can we go?' asked Anita.

'It's not just that it's dangerous,' said Steve. 'We don't want to disturb the wildlife either. Too many people around wouldn't be good for them.'

We couldn't argue with that. Protecting the animals was more important than getting to set up the cameras, even if I really wanted to.

'There is a hide close by that you could wait in and watch for animals while we set up the cameras,' suggested Rhyah.

'What's a hide?' Anita asked.

'It's a hidden building that's safe from the wildlife where you can look out,' explained Adi.

'Are you happy to do that?' said Rhyah. 'Julia and Steve can wait with you.'

'**YES!**' we all said.

A hide sounds amazing! And maybe if we're lucky we'll even see the tigers walk past.

The hide, that afternoon
Guess what? I'm writing this from **INSIDE** the hide!

The hide was near the bottom of a slope. It was covered in vines and leaves and blended in to the jungle. I didn't even realise we'd arrived at first. It had a secret key hole behind a wooden block that Steve pushed aside. Inside, it was dark except for some slits and small windows in the walls that let in a bit of light.

We each stationed ourselves next to a window and I got out my adventure notebook. I was ready and determined to be as still and quiet as possible so that we could see any animal that walked past!

'Uh-oh,' said Leo next to me. He had frozen and was looking down at his walking boot. 'I didn't check my boots this morning for creepy crawlies.'

A **GIANT** spider was climbing out of the top of his boot, by the laces.

'Get it out get it out get it out!' said Leo frantically.

Steve kneeled down and untangled the spider from Leo's laces.

'Is it OK?' Leo was crying, tears streaming down his face.

'Oh Leo, don't worry!' said Steve. 'It's not poisonous or anything and it's gone now.'

'It's not that,' said Leo. 'I almost squashed it! I can't believe I almost squashed it!'

'But you didn't,' said Julia, trying to cheer him up.

Anita and I decided to double check our walking boots but luckily our boots were creepy crawly free.

We all settled back at our windows, and after a while of watching and not seeing anything, Leo spotted something.

'Come and see.' He beckoned to us, speaking softly. 'Look, it's a rabbit.'

'That's a gigantic rabbit,' I said. 'It must be a hare.'

We all watched as it hopped away.

Then we all sat down at our windows again and watched and waited. And waited. And **WAITED**!

And even though all I wanted was to get up and go looking for Tara the tiger cub, I was the stillest and quietest I'd ever been in my life. Ms Perry would have been very proud.

'I've been thinking,' whispered Leo to me and Anita. 'We're on the outskirts of the wildlife sanctuary, right?'

I nodded, looking out of my window to the

118

right. 'The bit of unprotected land is just over there.' Julia had pointed it out earlier.

'So there could be poachers, or traps, wild animals or anything out there, right?' asked Leo.

'I guess,' replied Anita.

'I think I want to go back to the tiger reserve,' whispered Leo. 'I'm scared of poachers.'

Steve overheard. 'Don't worry, we're safe in the hide. No one will even know that we're here.'

'Are you sure?' asked Leo.

'Positive,' said Steve.

'Listen,' said Julia, raising her finger to her lips.

I straightened my back and listened really hard, hoping she had heard a tiger roar. Eventually I heard the swish of something large moving through the jungle, branches cracking and grasses flattening underneath large feet.

'It must be elephants heading towards the

water,' Julia whispered. 'Did you know they can smell water from several miles away?'

'Wow,' I said, listening as the sound got louder and then quieter as they passed us. I looked out of the window but they weren't close enough to see, only to hear. Then I heard something else. The rumble of thunder.

I looked at Julia. She opened the door and stared at the sky.

'I don't want to get our hopes up but there could be rain coming!' she said.

Almost as soon as she finished speaking, it started **POURING**. Huge droplets hammered on the roof. I was glad we were safely inside. Then I thought about the ride in the open top jeep home. That didn't seem like fun.

'Did anyone bring their raincoat?' asked Julia.

I shook my head.

'No,' said Leo.

'I almost did,' said Anita.

'Oh dear,' said Julia. 'It looks like we're going to get a bit wet.'

'This is wonderful for the animals though!' said Steve. 'What brilliant timing.'

And even though the thunder and lightning was scary and I knew that we were all going to get soaked, I was happy because this meant that all the animals were going to have water to drink again.

'Adi and Rhyah are going to be thrilled,' said Julia.

The rain outside continued to fall and fall and puddles gathered at the bottom of the slope around the hide. We were supposed to wait for Adi and Rhyah to come and fetch us once they'd finished placing the cameras, but Steve and Julia kept looking at the water and then glancing at each other nervously.

'I'm going to have a look outside,' said Steve.

When he opened the door, we saw it was flooding around the base of the hide.

'We're going to have to evacuate before we get stuck!' said Steve.

'You said we'd be safe in here,' said Leo to Steve.

'I didn't think about the fact that it might rain,' said Steve. 'We're safe from other things in here, just not flooding.'

Leo looked nervously out of the window. You could hardly see outside through the rain.

'There's no way I'm going outside,' said Leo. 'It looks more dangerous than ever.'

'We've got to,' said Julia.

'You can do it!' said Steve. 'We'll be right here with you, buddy.'

'Do we have to go?' I asked. 'We haven't seen Tara yet. Can't we wait a little bit longer?'

'I'm sorry Tilly, there's no time,' said Julia. 'The ground is flooding too quickly. We have to get out of here now!'

Everyone's packing their backpacks now to keep things dry so I'd better go. I'll check in when we're safely at the tiger reserve. Somehow, I'll try and keep this notebook dry!

The Thirteenth Adventure

Objective: Get back to the jeep and the Adventure Club HQ.

Obstacles: A monsoon storm, wild animals and **TONS** of rain.

The veranda, that evening

After we left the hide, we had to wade through water up to our knees! My legs were soaking but the water wasn't cold, it was almost warm. And it felt a little bit exciting to be trekking through the jungle in a **STORM!** Tiny streams of water formed and ran in all directions down the slope towards us.

'This way,' called Steve, who was leading us. It was hard to hear him over the rain. Julia walked at the back, behind us, in case one of us fell or got left behind. Ahead, what had been a dry river bed with just a trickle of water in it was now a river. I was slipping and sliding, covered in mud. I fell over and Anita held out her hand and helped me up.

'We're going to need to cross this river somehow,' Steve said, pausing to look at the water. 'I wonder how deep it is.'

'Er, Steve,' said Leo, pointing at the water.

'What's that?'

I followed his line of sight.

At first, I thought he was pointing at a log floating down the river. But then I realised that the log had two eyes and was moving in our direction.

'Is that a **CROCODILE?**' I asked.

'Everyone away from the water, now,' said Steve urgently.

We all shrieked and hid behind Julia and Steve.

'Oh no, oh no, oh no,' said Leo. 'I don't want to be eaten by a crocodile!'

My heart raced. The crocodile was so big it was **TERRIFYING**. I could imagine it going snap snap snap and eating us all up. Just like that. Dinner.

'No sudden movements,' said Julia. 'Let's all back away slowly.'

I clutched Anita and Leo's hands and we stepped backwards, then turned around and tried

to walk away calmly.

I glanced back and saw that the crocodile had stopped following us. It was mostly submerged under the water, watching us walk away.

PHEW!

'We're going to have to find another way to get to the jeep,' said Steve. Rain droplets dripped down his face and off the tip of his nose. 'Follow me!'

We walked in silence for a while, looking out for more crocodiles and focusing on not falling. I grabbed on to vines and branches when I could to stop myself from slipping.

Then all of a sudden, I heard a familiar swish of

large animals moving through the jungle.

Up ahead was a herd of elephants.

And they were heading straight for us!

'**QUICK!**' shouted Julia. 'Everyone out of the way!'

It was the closest I'd ever come to something that big. Three of the elephants had large tusks. The leader at the front flapped her ears as she walked and felt the earth with her trunk.

The elephants were bigger than ...

- The jeep.
- A hippo.
- My bedroom!

We raced deeper into the jungle out of the way of the elephants, flattening bushes with our feet. I was out of breath but we didn't stop moving until we were far, far away from them.

When we finally stopped, Steve and Julia

turned around on the spot, scanning the thick jungle around us. I recognised the look on their faces. It was the same one Mum had when she couldn't find our car in a huge car park.

'Are we lost?' I asked.

'We're not lost,' said Julia. 'It's just going to take me a second to get our bearings.'

Steve was trying to get his phone to work but it was getting drenched.

'Would now be a good time to use my whistle?' asked Leo.

'It would be a great time to use your whistle,' said Julia. 'Hopefully Adi and Rhyah will hear it.'

Leo raised it to his lips and blew. The high-pitched sound cut through the rain and thunder.

Over the storm I heard another sound.

'What's that noise?' asked Anita. 'It sounded like a bark. Oh no, I bet it's wolves isn't it?'

'Don't worry,' I said. 'Wolves don't sound like that, they howl.'

Although on the inside I was scared too. The sound could be coming from a dangerous animal I didn't know!

'We're definitely going to get eaten by **SOMETHING** out here, aren't we?' said Leo.

'Of course we're not. Blow your whistle again,' said Steve.

Leo blew it and we all stayed silent, listening for the strange sound. And then we heard it!

'It's the jeep horn!' said Julia. 'Let's follow that sound!'

I let out the biggest sigh of relief.

Leo and his whistle led us back to Rhyah and Adi.

I was so happy to see them. And even happier to see the jeep that was parked right behind them. Even the rain was easing off!

We all climbed inside the jeep, laughing and soaking wet. I squeezed the water out of my hair. It was dusk and the sky was darkening.

'Does everyone's head torch still work?' asked Julia. 'Now would be a good time to put them on.'

We were all silent as we drove away. I leant my head against Anita's, relieved that we were all OK, but sad that we hadn't found Tara the tiger. She could still be in the unprotected land or stuck crossing the busy road.

'The waterhole's just over there,' said Adi, pointing to our right. 'We set up all the cameras.'

I smiled a little at that. At least Adi and Rhyah managed to place the cameras before the rain. There was only one more full day before we left to find Tara and make sure that she was safe.

Just then a **HUGE** bat flew above my head and I jumped. It was **SCARY** going through the jungle at night. The trees looked different and I thought that every shadow was a leopard or a jackal.

'It's going to be bumpy for a minute,' shouted Rhyah from the driver's seat. 'Hold on!'

The jeep went up and down a muddy bank and we slid into each other on the back seat. The engine revved and the jeep lurched forward and then stopped moving. The wheels rolled and rolled as Rhyah tried to move the jeep, but we were going nowhere. We were stuck in the mud.

The Fourteenth Adventure

   Objective: Free the jeep.

   Obstacles: The thick, sticky mud!

'We're going to have to get out and push,' said Adi.

We all clambered out of the jeep, our feet

squelching in thick mud.

I plodded through the mud to the front of the jeep to see how bad it was. My head torch lit up the way. The front tyres were buried deep in the mud. When Rhyah pressed down on the accelerator the wheels spun round and round, going nowhere, flinging mud everywhere.

I turned around to help everyone push and saw something that made me freeze.

A pair of eyes shone back at me through the darkness.

My heart skipped a beat.

Could it be Tara?

I shone the torch ahead to get a better view. It was a tiger cub! Orange with black stripes. It turned away from me and splashed playfully in a big puddle.

It looked just like Tara, like this:

She had huge paws that seemed too big for her body, cute round ears and a fluffy face. She prowled forwards, towards me, and I saw the triangle of white fur over her eyebrows. And then I saw something else.

Another pair of cat's eyes reflected the torch light. A much larger tiger was swimming in a pool of water next to her. Its huge and muscular head was sticking out above the water. Tara's mum.

Rhyah was about to rev the engine and I spun

around and held my arm up in a stop sign. She saw and opened the door.

'Everything OK?' she whispered.

'Look,' I said, and pointed at Tara and her mother.

'Tilly, come back in the jeep,' said Rhyah. 'We can watch safely from there.' She called softly to everyone else to come back in the car as well.

I tore my eyes away for a few seconds to get back in the jeep.

The storm was passing and the moon peeked out from behind the clouds, giving us a clear view of the tigers. The mum kept an eye on us the whole time while Tara played with the water, pouncing, splashing and swimming. After what felt like ages, the mum nudged Tara onwards and they disappeared into the night, their tails swishing behind them.

'That was **AMAZING!**' I said.

'The best!' said Anita.

'Are they in the protected area?' I asked Rhyah.

'Yes,' replied Rhyah as she gazed after them.

'The tigers made it safely here and now they have drinking water,' I said, bouncing up and down in the back seat. 'Hooray!'

'That was even worth almost getting eaten by a crocodile,' said Leo.

We laughed.

My whole body tingled with excitement from seeing Tara the tiger cub and her mum.

Then we had to dig the mud out from around the tyres, but we're back at HQ now. We're all dry and recovering from our adventures with mango smoothies.

I still can't believe that I saw Tara the tiger cub and that she's OK! I think it was the best moment of **MY ENTIRE LIFE.**

The rooftop, that evening

After dinner it stopped raining and Leo, Anita
and I climbed on to the flat rooftop of the main
building to look at the stars. We sat down on a
wicker bench and leant against each other. There
were no sounds of traffic, just the noises of bugs
and animals and the warm wind rustling through
the trees. Above us, stars twinkled. I thought
about Tara the tiger cub out there with her mum,
wild and safe.

'A shooting star!'
said Leo, pointing as it
streaked through the sky.

'I wonder where we'll
be this time next year,'
said Anita.

That made me think about where Tara would be
next year. What if the monsoon was late again?

'What's the matter?' asked Leo, watching me.

'What if the monsoon is late again next year? More tigers might get lost or caught by poachers. It could even happen to Tara.'

'I hadn't thought of that,' said Anita sadly.

I rested my head back and thought about the tigers. I wished there was a way for them to get from the tiger reserve to the next protected area without worrying about crossing roads or encountering poachers. I wanted Tara to be safe always.

Day four, the LAST full day
The veranda, afternoon

I woke up yawning and tired. I'd hardly slept a wink because I'd been trying to figure out a way to help the tigers next year too, but I hadn't had any brilliant ideas. I asked everyone about it at breakfast.

'Well, we have been planning a travel corridor

for the elephants and tigers to walk along, to get from one protected area to the other,' said Rhiyah.

'And now that we know where all the animals go and the route that they take,' continued Adi, 'we know where would be best to build it.'

'That's a great idea!' I said. 'How do we do that?'

'First we have to mark the travel corridor out with rope and markings,' said Rhyah. 'We need to make sure the route is safe for the animals to get from here to the waterhole, so we'll have to avoid the village, the road and watch out for poachers.'

'How long will that take?' I asked.

'A while!' said Adi.

'Even with three extra helpers?' I asked, tilting my head to the side. 'We've got one whole day left.'

'Make that five extra helpers,' said Steve. 'Julia and I will help too!'

'Well then, let's get started!' said Adi, and he

clapped his hands together.

The Fifteenth Adventure

Objective: Build a protected wildlife corridor.

Obstacles: Marking out the path – it's long!

We gathered supplies and piled into the jeep. We were going to mark out the exact route that Tara the tiger cub and her mum had taken to get to the waterhole. We drove to the first village we knew they'd been near, parked, and all got out. We had to continue the rest of the way on foot.

'It's still muddy!' said Leo, stepping into a puddle.

It was hot and I was soon sweating and sticky.

'Once the route is marked out, we'll ask the government to turn it into part of the Big Tiger Reserve. Then humans will know not to go there or build roads that cross it, and the animals can travel safely,' said Rhyah. She smiled as I nodded hopefully.

Anita, Leo and I marked the trail by tying rope between trees and painting numbers on tree trunks. We had to make sure that the corridor was large enough for a whole herd of elephants to walk along.

'This is going to take ages!' said Anita.

'I know,' I said. 'But it's going to be worth it!'

It took us all day just to reach a **QUARTER** of the way to the waterhole in the protected area.

'There's still lots to do, but we've made a great start,' said Julia, standing back to admire our work. 'Well done, everyone!'

I nodded. Now that it was started, it would be ready in time for next year and then the tigers won't have to leave the safety of the Big Tiger Reserve to go and find water. Trekking through the jungle was exhausting and my body ached but I was proud of what we'd done.

Now I just have to wait a **WHOLE YEAR** to see if the wildlife corridor gets used. Usually having to wait that long would send me into a tizzy, but I'm trying to remember that it will be something to look forward to. (That's what Mum said to do about the next Adventure Club trip being **SO** far away.) I'm smiling as I think about the next year. With all the Adventure Club trips we have planned, it's going to be the best year yet!

Day five, morning, the jeep

After breakfast, it was time for goodbyes because our flight was leaving later that day. First, we said goodbye to Mo and Mishka. I stroked their trunks and whispered goodbye into their ears. I think they're the two **CUTEST** elephants in the world.

Then I said thank you to Rhyah and Adi for everything.

'I'll send you the pictures from the cameras we set up at the waterhole,' said Adi.

'Brilliant,' I said.

'We'd like to thank you for your help,' said Rhyah to us all. 'You worked really hard.'

I smiled proudly. 'It was worth it to know that Tara the tiger cub is safe and sound.'

We waved goodbye from our last ride in the jeep and I hoped that I'd get to visit again one day, maybe when Tara and I are both grown-ups.

On the Adventure Club jet, several hours later
Now we're on the plane. I can't believe we're going home already! I'm going to miss Tara the tiger cub. Before we take off, I whisper goodbye to her from the plane and imagine her playing in the water with her mum.
I look at Anita and Leo snoring next to me in their

seats. I'm going to miss them so much too, but we've already made a plan to meet up soon, even though we live far away from each other!

Home, two days later

This morning I woke up very, **VERY** early. It wasn't even fully light yet! Mum said that my body clock was wonky from all the travelling.

Marigold wanted to go outside, so I opened the back door and went to look at the stars. If I squinted, I could almost pretend that I was back in the jungle, watching for animals.

A second later it felt like I really was back there, because I spotted a creature! It was bumbling towards our garden shed!

I peeked underneath the shed and saw a **HEDGEHOG**.

I'm so excited that we have a hedgehog in our garden. It's got me thinking of a new project for the Afterschool Adventure Club ...

The Sixteenth Adventure

   Objective: Come up with a new project for the Afterschool Adventure Club.

   Obstacles: Not knowing much about hedgehogs!

The kitchen, later that day

Julia has just emailed the photos from the wildlife pictures at the waterhole and I've printed them out for my notebook!

I can't believe that all those animals are drinking from the waterhole together. Charlotte is coming over in a bit and I can't wait to show her!

My bedroom, that evening

Charlotte loved looking at the photographs and she showed me some of hers from her camping trip in return.

'I've got an idea for the Afterschool Adventure Club project,' I told her. 'I've been reading about hedgehogs and how they need to be able to get into people's gardens at night in order to eat enough food. But too many gardens are fenced in. We'd have to ask the owners' permission, of course, and then we could build corridors and holes in the fences for the hedgehogs to go through.'

'I love it!' said Charlotte and her face lit up. 'The same way you were building a wildlife corridor for the elephants and tigers in India!'

'Exactly,' I said. 'A hedgehog highway!'

The library, the next day

Charlotte and I have done lots of research.

We've found out that hedgehogs:

- Can hibernate.
- Are nocturnal.
- Walk over two miles foraging in a night.
- Are actually lactose intolerant, so they can't drink milk. But they do like water!
- Are good for the garden because they eat pests like slugs.
- Like to rest in compost heaps or bonfire piles.
- Are most likely to be seen on a summer evening.

We made a little information page and printed it out. Then we designed some stickers that said **HEDGEHOG HIGHWAY** for people to put over their holes. Mum had said that she could make them from waterproof vinyl.

'That way, everyone can know what the hole is for,' I said.

Charlotte nodded.

'We can share it with everyone at the Afterschool Adventure Club,' said Charlotte.

'Perfect!' I said and we high-fived each other.

Willow-house HQ, the next week

Today was the first Afterschool Adventure Club meeting after the summer holidays. The willow-house had grown so much over summer that you could hardly see in through the thick leaves.

The first thing I did was inspect the school bee and butterfly garden. Everything was still in bloom and the gardener had left me a note which said:

Hi, Afterschool Adventure Club,
I kept an eye out for the purple emperor, the rare butterfly. I didn't see it but I did see lots of painted lady butterflies and peacock butterflies so you can add them to your list. Maybe you'll see the rare one next year!
From,
Janet

Just as I was reading the note, a peacock butterfly landed on the purple lavender!

Back in the willow-house, everyone loved the idea of building hedgehog highways.

'We can build some in the school fence and next week we can organise a camp out to see if we can spot a hedgehog,' said Ms Perry.

Everyone buzzed with excitement. We got to work straight away preparing the handouts to post through people's letterboxes.

We set off in a group to deliver the hedgehog highway info. I linked arms with Charlotte and we led the way.

Back at school, we carefully measured a hole to go in the fence, then we drew it on in pen and watched as Ms Perry cut it out.

Afterwards, we attached our **HEDGEHOG HIGHWAY** sign and stood back to admire our work.

'I hope it gets used tonight!' said Charlotte.

'I wish that we could see it tonight too,' I said hopefully, turning to smile at Ms Perry.

She laughed. 'You'll have to be patient and wait until next week, Tilly. I need to get all your parents' permissions.'

I sighed. It was a good thing that I was getting so great at being patient, because I was having to wait **A LOT!**

Willow-house HQ, the next week
Tonight, the whole Afterschool Adventure Club is squeezed into the willow-house, watching the Hedgehog Highway through the leaves! It's been two hours and we haven't seen anything yet, but we have eaten lots of yummy snacks. We left out a bowl of water for the hedgehog and some special hedgehog food to tempt it to come this way. Oh — Mo says he sees something — I've got to go!

A few minutes later ...

We saw a **HEDGEHOG!** It bumbled up to the highway and poked its nose through and sniffed, and then it stepped through the hole and tucked into the food right away, just like this:

Everyone made 'aww' noises. It was **VERY** cute. Charlotte grasped my hand excitedly and smiled at me. The hedgehog hung out in our school garden for a while and then it disappeared off through the hedge on the other side!

I can't believe how many wonderful adventures I got to have this summer. I found Tara the tiger and her mum, bathed and fed elephants calves, started a wildlife corridor in India **AND** made a wildlife highway at home too! There were some moments when it felt like the waiting was **TOO** much to handle, but I've learnt that's part of the adventure as well! And sometimes when you've waited ages for something, it's even more amazing when it happens, like how finally seeing Tara the tiger cub was pretty much the best moment of my entire life.

I'm almost out of space to write so I think it's time for a new notebook. Which means I'll have to find some new adventures too! Until next time ...

Tilly

How to build a hedgehog highway

Did you know that British hedgehogs are declining in numbers and vulnerable to extinction? Hedgehogs travel through gardens and parks every night looking for food. They eat slugs and pests which makes them the perfect garden visitor.

Do you have a garden that is enclosed by a fence? If you do, you can build a hedgehog highway so that they can continue on their way! Make sure you ask your parents for help and get together with your neighbours to ask their permission before you begin.

To build a hedgehog highway, you will need:

A fence or a fence panel

Ruler

Pencil

A saw

Sandpaper

What to do:

1. Think about where a hedgehog might like to enter and leave your garden. Make sure the hole doesn't lead out on to a busy road.

2. Measure a square 13cm by 13cm at the bottom of your fence and draw the outline with the pencil. This size is perfect for hedgehogs but too small for most pets to get through.

3. Have an adult help you use the saw to cut along the pencil lines.

4. Sandpaper along any rough edges.

Then your hedgehog highway is ready to go!

If you don't have a garden, you can also help a hedgehog by:

- Making a log, twig or leaf pile, or a compost heap as a hedgehog house!
- Leaving out a shallow dish of water.
- Picking up litter – empty bottles, cartons and plastic bags are very dangerous to hedgehogs.
- Checking bonfires for hedgehogs before they're lit, and areas of long grass before mowing the lawn or strimming.

The best time to see a hedgehog is in the early morning or evening as they are nocturnal, which means they sleep during the day. Hedgehogs hibernate in nests of leaves or undergrowth from November until March.

Look out for more of Tilly's adventures in her next books!

POLAR BEAR PATROL
THE ORPHAN ORANGUTAN

JESS BUTTERWORTH

Jess was born in London and spent her childhood between the UK and India. She studied creative writing at Bath Spa University and is the author of many books for children. She's filled *The Adventure Club* series with all the things she loved as a child (and still loves to this day!).